Who Is Your Favorite Monster, MAMA?

By **BARBARA SHOOK HAZEN**

Illustrated by **MARYANN KOVALSKI**

HYPERION BOOKS FOR CHILDREN
NEW YORK

First Edition

10 9 8 7 6 5 4 3 2 1

Printed in Singapore

Library of Congress Cataloging-in-Publication Data on file.

Designed by Elizabeth H. Clark

ISBN 0-7868-1810-7

Reinforced binding

Visit www.hyperionbooksforchildren.com

For my favorite son, Brack, and my favorite grand-
child, Katie, with monstrous love
—B.S.H.

For my favorite monsters—Yenno, Betty Lou, and D.
—M.K.

HARRY was happy when his mama crooned,

"Euuu, my cute little monster child,

I love the way you warm my wild.

I love your warts and baby bristles.

I love your nails as soft as thistles.

I love your fangs and furry nose.

I love you, Harry, head to toes."

Harry was happy when he called,
"MAMACOMENOW!"
and Mama Monster came on the
quick with just what he wanted.

Harry was not happy when he called, **"MAMACOMENOW!"** and Mama Monster called back, "CAN'T! I'm busy with your big brother, Bruxley,"

or "LATER! I have to burp your baby sister, Bronwen."

Harry had three pet creepy beasties—
a mole, a slug, and a bat. He tamed them
and named them Tiny, Slimy, and Whiny.

Harry's creepy beasties shared his pillow slab, licked his hurts, and listened when he fretted, "Why does Mama Monster have more time for Bruxley and Bronwen than for me?"

One day, Harry Monster built a tower with the help of his creepy beasties. Each helped in its own special way. Tiny gnawed, Slimy glued, and Whiny tacked the top pieces in place.

When it was finished, Harry called,

"MAMACOMESEE!"

When Mama Monster didn't come on the quick,
Harry felt a stab of mad.

He tromped into the living den, where Mama Monster
was eyeballing the wall and smacking her lips.

"Isn't Bronwen's quicksand painting frightfully delightful?" she said.

"No!" said Harry.

"And isn't Bruxley's frosted fly pie delicious?" she said as she handed Harry a glob.

"**NO!**"

Harry growled and hurled his glob at Bronwen's painting.

"You never want to see what *I* do," he sulked. "And you don't love me anymore."

"Euuu, but I do," Mama Monster said,
"as much as a mountain, as wide as outside,
and deeper every day, even when you are
sulky and snarly."

Mama Monster then took Harry's paw and said,
"Now, show me what you did."

When she saw his tower, she clapped and cackled,
"FANTABULOUS!"

This made Harry happy until . . .

. . . he overheard Mama Monster call Bruxley
"my huge helper" for creative celery chopping,
which Harry was told he was too little to do,

and he overheard her call Bronwen "horribly adorable"
for crayoning "I ♥ MAMA" on the tablecloth, which
Harry was told he was too old to do.

Hearing them praised made Harry seethe with envy.
He grabbed a can of flea powder and sprinkled it on
Bruxley's celery pile.

Then he tweaked Bronwen's toes till she hollered,
"HARRYOWWWW!"

"I'm disappointed in you," Mama Monster told Harry, and sent him to his bed slab to think things over.

Harry lay there muttering, "Nobody loves me anymore."

"We do! We do!" His creepy beasties tried to comfort him. Slimy cooled his brow, Whiny fanned his forehead, and Tiny whisker-kissed his fangs.

"Mama Monster doesn't," Harry sobbed.

"Euuu, but I do," Mama Monster said as she came in and sat next to Harry, "as much as a mountain, as wide as outside, and deeper every day, even when you are mean, green jealous."

"As much as Bronwen and Bruxley?" Harry had to know.
"As much as Bronwen and Bruxley," said Mama Monster and she fondled Harry's fangs.

Harry felt better, but he still wasn't satisfied. He sighed, took a deep, brave breath, and asked the question that itched his insides.

"Who is your favorite monster, Mama? Who do you love most?"

"Why, I . . . I don't know." Mama Monster twiddled her chins and stared into space, stumped.

After long thought, she asked Harry, "Who is your favorite creepy beastie? Who do you love most?

"Tiny?

"Slimy?

"Or Whiny?"

"Silly question!" Harry bristled and clutched them close. "Each is my most favorite because each is frightfully, delightfully different. I love each the most but not the same."

"What a smart answer. And just the one I was looking for!" Mama Monster snorted for joy. "Euuu, I am so proud of you. For sure and forever, you are my most loved Harry Monster."

This made Harry so horribly
happy, he hugged his mama,

kissed Bronwen's toes,

took a tiny bite of
Bruxley's latest concotion,

and skipped out to savor the day.